Kayla
the Pottery
Fairy

ISBN 978-0-545-70829-6

12 11 10 9 8 7 6 5 4 3 2 1   15 16 17 18 19 20/0

Printed in the U.S.A.   40

This edition first printing, March 2015

Kayla
the Pottery
Fairy

by Daisy Meadows

SCHOLASTIC INC.

The Fairyland Palace

Sara Sketchley's house

Bridge

Maze

Park

Rainspell

Island

Carrie's Jewelry Shop

Beach and Boardwalk

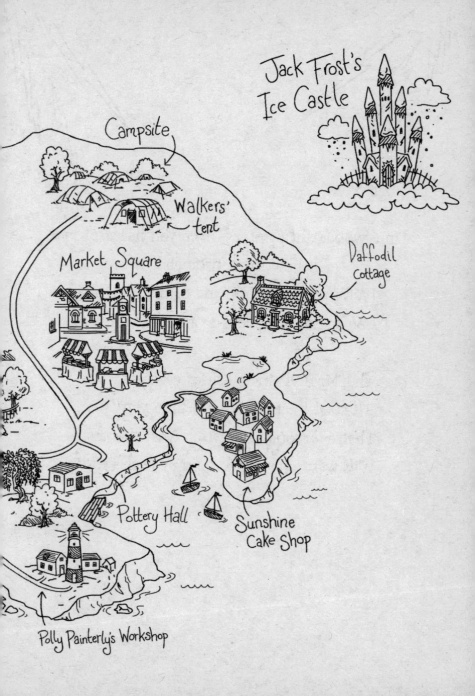

Jack Frost's
Ice Castle

Campsite

Walkers'
tent

Market Square

Daffodil
Cottage

Pottery Hall

Sunshine
Cake Shop

Polly Painterly's Workshop

I'm a wonderful painter—have you heard of me?
Behold my artistic ability!
With palette, brush, and paints in hand,
I'll be the most famous artist in all the land!

The Magical Crafts Fairies can't stop me!
I'll steal their magic, and then you'll see
That everyone, no matter what the cost,
Will want a painting done by Jack Frost!

Contents

Crafts Week

"I can see Rainspell Island!" Rachel
Walker cried as the ferry sailed across
the blue-green sea, foamy waves slapping
against its sides. Up ahead was a rocky
island with soaring cliffs and sandy
golden beaches. Rachel turned to her
best friend, Kirsty Tate, with a smile.
"It's not far now."

"Aren't we lucky, Rachel?" Kirsty asked, her face bright with excitement. "We visited here not that long ago for the music festival, and now we're back again for Crafts Week!"

"And maybe some fairy adventures, too?" Rachel whispered hopefully.

"Maybe . . . if we're *really* lucky," said Kirsty with a grin.

The girls had met for the first time on Rainspell Island on vacation with their families. While exploring the island together, they'd made an amazing discovery—they'd found a tiny fairy named Ruby! Ever since then, Rachel and Kirsty had been loyal friends of the fairies. The girls had helped their magical friends many times when selfish Jack Frost and his goblins were causing chaos in Fairyland.

The ferry docked at the pier, and the girls' parents came up from below deck with all of their bags.

"That's our taxi," said Mr. Tate, pointing out a car waiting on the pier.

"Mom said you can come and stay

with us at the b and b for a few nights,
Rachel," Kirsty said as they left the ferry.

"And you can come and stay at the
campsite with us," Rachel added eagerly.
"It'll be fun!"

Once the bags had been loaded into
the taxi, the driver headed for Daffodil
Cottage, the bed and breakfast where
the Tates were
staying. As they
drove up, Rachel
noticed that
Rainspell Island
was looking
especially green
and gorgeous. It
was spring, and the
wildflowers were in full bloom.

Before long, they arrived at Daffodil

Cottage, a pretty little house with a thatched roof.

"Mom, can I go over to the campsite with Rachel?" Kirsty asked as the taxi driver unloaded their bags.

"Of course," Mrs. Tate replied. "We'll come and pick you up later."

The campsite was a little farther down the road in a large field. When they arrived, Rachel and Kirsty jumped out of the taxi, thrilled to see that Mr. and Mrs. Walker had rented one of the biggest tents on the site.

"Look, Kirsty, it's just like a canvas house!" Rachel said, running around the tent. "There are separate bedrooms *and* a living room."

"Cool!" Kirsty laughed, just as excited. "We can have a midnight dance party without waking up your mom and dad."

"Rachel, why don't you and Kirsty head into town and find out more about Crafts Week?" Mrs. Walker suggested. "Your dad and I will unpack."

"OK," Rachel agreed.

"There's an information booth in the town square," Mr. Walker told the girls. "The organizers will be able to tell you exactly what's happening this week."

The girls left the tent and hurried across the field. The town wasn't very far away at all—in fact, they could see the rooftops in the distance. They climbed over a small

fence and then wandered down a twisty
country lane.

"I always get the feeling that
something magical is going to happen on
Rainspell," Kirsty said dreamily.

"That's because it always does!"
Rachel laughed.

The girls had been to town many times before, so they found their way to the square easily. It was very busy, with lots of families milling around. In the middle of the square was a large red-and-white striped tent with RAINSPELL ISLAND CRAFTS WEEK embroidered on it in gold letters.

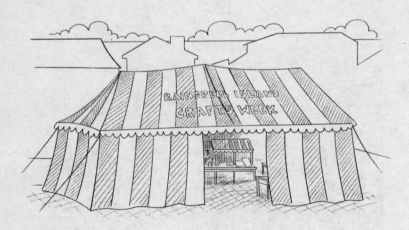

It was even busier inside the tent. There was a long line of people waiting to speak to the organizer, who stood behind a table piled with pamphlets. She was handing them out as fast as she could, so the girls joined the end of the line to patiently wait their turn.

"Hello, girls! How can I help you?" the woman asked when Rachel and Kirsty finally reached the table. She was wearing a name badge that said ARTEMIS JOHNSON.

"Hello, Miss Johnson," Kirsty said politely. "My friend Rachel and I would like some information about Crafts Week."

"Please call me

Artie!" The woman beamed at them.
"Now, are you interested in any
particular activities?"

"We're staying here for the whole
week, so we want to try *everything*,"
Rachel explained.

"Fantastic!" Artie replied. "The
activities are taking place all over the
island, so here's a map to show you
where." She handed the map to Kirsty.
"There's a pottery class in the hall down
by the pier. You can make
jewelry at the
accessories store and
learn to bake at the
cookie shop, and
lots more!"

The girls glanced
at each other in

delight. They hardly knew where to
start!

"Oh, and at the end of the week there
will be a special outdoor exhibition,"
Artie added. "Everyone who has
participated in Crafts Week can enter
something they've made, and we'll be
giving out prizes."

"That sounds great! Thanks, Artie,"
said Rachel.

"Before you go, take a look at our
arts-and-crafts display." Artie gestured
at a table on the other side of the tent.
"Everything there has been made by our
professional Crafts Week instructors."

The girls went over to take a look.
The centerpiece on the table was a
magnificent strawberry shortcake that
made Kirsty's mouth water just looking

at it. The cake was surrounded by paintings of wildflowers and pencil sketches of Rainspell Island, alongside a patchwork quilt, delicate silver jewelry, and handmade books. There was also a display of curvy clay pots coated with a shiny blue glaze.

"I'd love to learn how to make a clay pot," Kirsty said to Rachel.

"I think it's called *throwing* a pot," Rachel said with a grin. "Or maybe that's just what you do if you make a mistake!"

"Hello, girls," said a tiny voice out of nowhere. "Would you like to have even *more* magical crafts fun?"

Art
Attack!

At first, Rachel and Kirsty were startled.
Then they both smiled from ear to
ear—a little fairy was peeking over the
rim of one of the shiny blue pots! She
waved happily at them.

"I'm Kayla the Pottery Fairy," she
explained, her eyes twinkling cheerfully.

15

She looked very pretty in her denim shirtdress, cropped gray leggings, and pink shoes. "I'm one of the seven Magical Crafts Fairies, and I'm here to invite you to a *very* special event in Fairyland. Would you like to come?"

"Yes, please!" the girls cried in unison. Even though they'd visited Fairyland many times, it was still a huge thrill to go back!

Kayla tumbled out of the pot and fluttered underneath the table, hidden from view by the folds of the tablecloth. Rachel and Kirsty quickly ducked under the table, too. Then, with one flick of her wand, Kayla's

glittery magic whirled them all away to
Fairyland.

A few magical seconds later, the girls
found themselves surrounded by the
familiar toadstool houses of Fairyland.
They'd landed in the middle of a huge
crowd of fairies clustered around a
podium that had been set up on the
riverbank. Queen Titania and King

Oberon were on the podium, seated on their golden thrones. Bertram, their frog footman, stood nearby. Then Kirsty noticed a silver banner strung above the podium. MAGICAL CRAFTS WEEK was painted on it in scarlet letters.

Kirsty was amazed. "You're having a Crafts Week, too, Kayla?" she said.

"We are!" Kayla grinned. "It's organized by me and the other Magical Crafts Fairies. Why don't you come and meet them? We're just waiting for Queen Titania and King Oberon to open Crafts Week."

Kayla led the way through the crowd toward the podium. The girls followed, waving and calling hello as they spotted lots of their old friends.

In front of the podium, six fairies were having a serious discussion.

"Girls, these are the other Magical Crafts Fairies," Kayla said, pointing her wand at each of them in turn. "Annabelle the Drawing Fairy, Zadie the Sewing Fairy, Josie the Jewelry Fairy, Violet the Painting Fairy, Libby the Writing Fairy, and Roxie the Baking Fairy."

"Welcome to Magical Crafts Week, girls!" the fairies said all together, smiling.

"I'm sure you've already guessed that it's our job to make sure that crafts are fun in both the human and the fairy worlds," Roxie added.

"All the fairies will be trying out lots of different crafts this week, just like you," Kayla told Rachel and Kirsty. "At the end of the week, Queen Titania and King Oberon will pick the best, most beautiful things and use them to decorate their palace!"

At that moment, Bertram hopped to the front of the podium. "Silence for their Royal Majesties, King Oberon and Queen Titania," he proclaimed.

The king and queen stepped forward. "Welcome, one and all, to our Magical Crafts Week," the queen said. "I see that some special friends have come to join us!" She directed a sweet smile at the girls.

Suddenly, to her surprise, Rachel spotted a green balloon sailing over the crowd. The balloon was heading straight for the podium! Before Rachel knew what was happening, it hit the floor next to Queen Titania and exploded, splattering bright green paint all over her sparkling silver gown. Everyone in the crowd gasped, and the queen cried out in distress.

"What's happening?" Rachel cried. She and Kirsty ducked as more paint-filled balloons zoomed toward the podium. These balloons burst near the Magical Crafts Fairies, covering them in green paint, too!

Each of the Magical Crafts Fairies had been holding her special magic object, but they set them down on the grass as they attempted to clean themselves up. Just then, Kirsty spotted a familiar, icy figure striding through the crowd.

"We should have guessed, Rachel!"

Kirsty groaned. "It's Jack Frost!"

Grinning with glee, Jack Frost headed for the podium. Rachel noticed that he had a big leather bag hanging on his frosty shoulder. Behind him, a group of goblins hurled more paint-filled balloons in every direction. Some of the fairies ran for cover, while others tried to catch the balloons before they popped.

In the middle of the chaos, Jack Frost jumped onto the podium. At that moment, the girls heard a shout from Kayla.

"Jack Frost stole all of our magic objects!" she cried.

"Of course I did!" Jack Frost sneered triumphantly. Rachel and Kirsty were shocked to see that he was clutching Kayla's vase, along with the six other magic objects. "After all, I'm the greatest artist ever! And I'm going to make sure that no one—fairy or human—uses these

objects to try to be better than *me*!"

Jack Frost shoved the vase and other objects into his bag, as the goblins charged onto the podium to join him. Then, with one sweep of his wand, Jack Frost created a bolt of icy blue magic that whisked him and the goblins away to the human world.

Clay Catastrophe

"This is a disaster!" King Oberon murmured, shaking his head. "Without the magic objects, crafting everywhere will be totally ruined!"

The Magical Crafts Fairies looked at each other miserably, their wings drooping.

"We can help," Kirsty piped up from the front of the crowd. "Right, Rachel?"

"Of course we can," Rachel agreed. "Jack Frost isn't going to get away with this!"

"Oh, girls, you're always here when we need you," Queen Titania said gratefully. "And the Magical Crafts Fairies will help you however they can."

Kayla wiped a splotch of green paint off her nose and beckoned to Rachel and Kirsty. "Let's get back to Rainspell Island right away, girls," she said urgently.

As Kayla waved her wand, Rachel and Kirsty felt her powerful magic

whisk them up, up, and away from
Fairyland. They could hear the other
fairies calling, "Good luck!" Just a
heartbeat later, the girls found themselves
outside the information booth in the
Rainspell Island town square. Kayla
immediately darted out of sight into
Rachel's pocket.

"Where should we start looking for
your vase?" Kirsty asked her.

"Jack Frost probably gave the magic
objects to his goblins to keep safe," Kayla
guessed. "The goblins who have my vase
will *definitely* want to do some pottery!"

"Artie said we could try pottery in the
hall down by the pier," Rachel reminded
Kirsty. "Let's look there first."

The girls checked the Crafts Week map
and then headed to the pier. On the way,

Rachel was surprised to see a group of angry people stomp by, complaining loudly to one another about what a terrible time they were having. Rachel could see that they were spattered with something that looked like mud—and they weren't the only ones! More people trailed along behind them, all covered with mud and all coming from the pier.

"I wonder what's going on?" Rachel remarked, scratching her head.

At that moment, a woman wearing a dirty leather apron came hurrying toward them. Kirsty noticed her name tag—MADELEINE POTTS, POTTERY INSTRUCTOR—and called out to her as she went by.

"Is everything OK?" Kirsty asked, concerned. "We were just on our way to your pottery class."

"I'd suggest you
wait a little while,
girls," Madeleine Potts
replied, sounding
exasperated. "Some
troublemaking boys
have been causing
complete chaos,
throwing clay at
everyone—including me!" She
looked down at her clay-stained
apron. "I'm going to get Artie to help
me get them out of the pottery hall."
Then she dashed off.

"Troublemaking boys?" Rachel
repeated. "Sounds more like
troublemaking goblins!"

"Let's go!" Kayla piped up excitedly

from Rachel's pocket.

The girls ran the rest of the way to the pottery hall. When they arrived, they could hear shrieks and giggles inside.

"Wait," Kirsty said as Rachel reached for the door handle. "Maybe Kayla could turn us into fairies before we go in. It'll be easier to stay out of sight."

"You're right!" Kayla replied with a wink. She fluttered out of Rachel's pocket, waved her wand, and surrounded the girls with a mist of sparkling magic. In no time at all, Rachel and Kirsty were the same size as Kayla, with delicate, translucent wings on their backs!

The three friends flew through an open window into the hall. There, to their surprise, they found themselves right in the middle of a storm of wet clay! Blobs of clay were flying through the air, and Rachel gave a yelp as one of them knocked her off balance and sent her into a nosedive. She flapped her wings hard and managed to zoom up again. Kayla and Kirsty both dodged from side to side, trying to avoid being hit by clay, too.

Kirsty glanced down and saw two goblins whooping with glee as they pelted each other with blob after blob of clay. Two more goblins had smeared clay all over the floor and were having fun sliding around as if they were on a skating rink.

"Madeleine Potts was right," Kirsty said breathlessly. "It's chaos in here!"

"Let's hide somewhere safe," Kayla suggested. "Then we can plan our next move." She flew down and ducked behind a vase that stood in the middle of the potter's wheel. Kirsty and Rachel followed. As they did, Kirsty noticed a shelf full of beautiful pots, vases, and jars nearby that were coated with bright, swirling glazes.

"Did the goblins make those?" Kirsty whispered, pointing to the shelf.

"Probably," Kayla replied. "The magic from my special vase means they've become expert potters!" She frowned. "My vase is here somewhere. I can *feel* it. . . ."

Rachel stared at the shelf, wondering if the goblins had hidden Kayla's magic vase there with the others. But then

Kayla gave a little squeal of excitement.

"Oh, girls, *look*!" she exclaimed, pointing. "Look at that green backpack on the workbench. See the faint magical glow around it?"

Rachel and Kirsty squinted at the open backpack. Inside was nestled a familiar, sparkly object— Kayla's vase!

"I have to get it back!" Kayla said, determined. "Wait here, girls." Without another word, she zoomed straight toward the backpack. Suddenly, a goblin in a clay-smeared apron came out of a nearby closet labeled STOREROOM, right near the backpack.

He was struggling, carrying a big and heavy block of clay. Kirsty and Rachel glanced at each other in dismay.

"Hurry, Kayla!" Kirsty murmured. Their fairy friend still hadn't realized the goblin was so close.

At first, the goblin seemed to be heading for the potter's wheel, but then he threw a casual glance at his backpack. He scowled as he spotted Kayla just about to dart inside. The goblin dropped the block of clay on the workbench and lunged at the little fairy!

"Kayla, look out!" Kirsty shouted.

In a Spin!

Kayla tried to get away, but it was too late. The goblin captured her in his clay-covered hands and held her tightly.

"Let me go!" Kayla demanded. "I just want my magic vase back."

"Well, you can't have it!" the goblin retorted. "I *love* pottery. See all these beautiful things I made?" He pointed proudly at the shelf. "No silly fairy is going to ruin my fun!"

Rachel and Kirsty watched from the potter's wheel as the goblin lifted the lid off one of the jars on the shelf. He dropped Kayla inside and put the lid on firmly.

"Kayla's trapped!" Rachel whispered, her eyes wide. "We have to rescue her, Kirsty."

But before the girls had time to come up with a plan, the goblin walked over to the potter's wheel and sat down to examine the vase he'd made earlier.

"This vase needs a little more work," he muttered to himself. He sat down on the stool and pressed his big green foot down hard on the operating pedal. The wheel immediately began to spin around and around, taking Rachel and Kirsty with it!

"Hold on, Kirsty!" Rachel gasped, clutching the edge of the wheel tightly. Kirsty did the same as the wheel went faster and faster.

After a moment or two, the girls were spinning so fast that

the room became a blur. They both
started to feel sick and dizzy! Soon, they
couldn't hold on any longer. Both Rachel
and Kirsty were thrown off the wheel, up
into the air! They
tumbled down into the
vase the goblin was
making and
landed on the
damp clay at the
bottom. The
girls both lay
there, unhurt
but dazed.

The goblin hadn't noticed
them. Luckily, just a few seconds later,
he brought the wheel to a stop.

"Thank goodness!" Rachel murmured.
"I'm so dizzy, I'm seeing double!"

"This clay is so wet and sticky," Kirsty complained, flicking a blob of it off one of her wings. Then Rachel saw her friend's eyes light up. "Oh!" Kirsty exclaimed. "That gave me an idea!"

Kirsty quickly whispered her plan to Rachel. Then, together, the two girls popped up out of the vase, just like Kayla had when they'd first met her. The goblin stared at them in disbelief, and then let out a shriek of rage.

"More fairies!" he roared. "I *hate* fairies! You're all annoying,

interfering, nosy little busybodies!"

"We just wanted to tell you how much we love your vase," Kirsty said with a sweet smile.

The goblin looked shocked. Then he grinned proudly.

"In fact, if your vase was a little bit taller, I'll bet you'd win one of the Crafts Week prizes," Rachel told him.

"Yes, I think I would, too—I'm

obviously the best potter on Rainspell Island!" the goblin bragged.

"If you stood on your stool, you'd be able to reach the top of the vase to make it taller," Kirsty pointed out innocently.

"You know, that's not a bad idea for a silly little fairy!" the goblin said. He hopped up onto the stool, stood on his tiptoes, and leaned over the vase. Kirsty and Rachel silently flew up behind him.

"Here we go, Rachel," Kirsty whispered. "On the count of three!"

Precious Pottery

"One, two, THREE!" whispered Kirsty. The girls zoomed toward the goblin and gave him a big push.

"Stop that!" the goblin yelled furiously, teetering back and forth on his stool. He lost his balance and fell headfirst into the vase in front of him! All the girls could see were his big, green feet sticking out of the top.

"Help!" came a muffled voice from inside the vase. Kirsty glanced over at the other goblins. They were still too busy playing with the clay to notice what was going on.

"Now to rescue Kayla!" Rachel said breathlessly. She and Kirsty flew over to the shelf as fast as their wings would take them.

"Which pot is she in?" asked Kirsty. But then they heard a tiny voice calling to them.

"Girls, girls, I'm inside the blue jar with the red lid!"

Together, Rachel and Kirsty found the jar and struggled to lift up the heavy lid. They managed to raise it just enough for Kayla to fly out. The little fairy looked very relieved, and gave them both a grateful hug.

"I see you figured out how to deal with the goblin!" Kayla whispered with a grin as she spotted his feet waving in the air. "Good job, girls. Now I can get my beautiful vase back!"

Kayla swooped toward the backpack. With one quick movement, she scooped up her vase and shrank it to fairy size. It shimmered with a wonderful, magic glow. Kayla tucked the little vase safely under her arm before

heading back to Rachel and Kirsty.

"Let's get out of here, girls," she began.
But suddenly the goblin inside the vase
hollered "HELP!" at the top of his
lungs.

This time, the
other goblins
heard him.
They turned
around, saw his feet
sticking out of the
vase, and dashed
toward him. But
the floor was wet and sticky with all the
clay they'd been throwing around, so the
goblins began slipping and sliding all
over the place! Shouting and squealing,
they crashed into the potter's wheel,
knocking the vase to the floor. Then

there was a heap of goblins flailing
around in a pile of wet clay, with the
goblin potter right in the middle.

"Oh, what a mess!" Kayla sighed.
One of the goblins heard her and
looked up. "That pesky fairy has her

magic vase back!" he pointed out, wiping a smear of clay off his nose. All of the goblins looked disappointed, but the one who had made the beautiful pots on the shelf looked saddest of all.

The goblins climbed to their feet and then, moaning and groaning about how angry Jack Frost was going to be, they trudged over to the door. The goblin potter hung back, taking a long, sad look at the pots he'd made.

Rachel and Kirsty exchanged a glance. Together, they fluttered over to the shelf and picked up a small but very pretty green pot, the only one they could lift between them. Then they flew over to the goblin and presented him with the pot.

"Oh!" The goblin's green face lit up. "Thank you!" He skipped out of the pottery hall, holding the pot as carefully as if it were precious treasure.

"Girls, you're so kind," Kayla said with a smile. "You made a goblin *and* a fairy extremely happy today— thank you a

thousand times over! I
can't wait to get
back to
Fairyland with
the fantastic
news. But first
I have a little
more work to do
here. . . ."

One flick of
Kayla's wand
returned Rachel and Kirsty to
their human size. A second burst of
magic fairy sparkles cleaned up the
pottery hall in the blink of an eye.
Whew!

"Someone's coming, girls," Kayla
whispered as voices came from outside
the hall. "I have to go. But I know you'll

be on the lookout for more of our magic objects!"

"We will, Kayla," Rachel cried. "Good-bye!"

"Good-bye," Kirsty echoed. The girls waved as Kayla vanished in a cloud of sparkly fairy dust.

Glittering Glazes

Just then, Madeleine Potts walked in with Artie. They both looked surprised to find the pottery hall empty except for the girls.

"Those boys must have left," Artie said, looking around. "You can continue your class now, Madeleine."

"Thank you so much for cleaning up, girls," Madeleine said gratefully as Artie left with a smile. "Would you like to try making some pots?"

"We'd love to!" Rachel replied.

Madeleine showed the girls how to knead, cut, and layer the clay to make it soft enough to work with. Then Kirsty began to roll lengths of clay to make a coil pot, while Madeleine taught Rachel how to use the potter's wheel.

"You're learning very quickly, Rachel," Madeleine said with a nod, watching as Rachel carefully molded a small pot on the spinning wheel. Rachel smiled. She didn't tell Madeleine that this wasn't her first experience with the potter's wheel that day!

More people wandered into the hall as

the girls prepared different-colored glazes
to use on their pots. Soon the whole
place was buzzing with laughter and
conversation. Madeleine was very busy
helping everyone with their clay
creations.

"I'll fire your pots in the kiln now, girls," she told Rachel and Kirsty. "Come back this afternoon, and they'll be ready for you. I'll add the glazes you've prepared."

"I can't wait to see them!" Rachel said
to Kirsty as they headed back to the
campsite for lunch.

Later that day, the girls rushed back to
the hall to collect their clay pots. They
were both giddy with excitement.
Madeleine was helping the last few
people finish their pots, but when she saw
Rachel and Kirsty, she hurried over to
them.

"I think you girls are going to be very happy!" Madeleine said, leading them over to a table filled with beautiful pots. At the front was Kirsty's coil pot, coated in a pink and purple glaze that sparkled just like Kayla's magic vase. Next to it was Rachel's hand-thrown pot, glazed in red and green, and glittering just as brightly.

"I don't know how you two managed to get your glazes to sparkle like that," Madeleine said admiringly, "but they look wonderful!"

Kirsty and Rachel exchanged a quick, secret smile. They knew it was fairy magic!

And even though they'd found Kayla's vase, the girls knew that this ·was only the beginning of their Crafts Week adventures. Six magic objects were still missing, and it was up to Rachel and Kirsty to bring them home to Fairyland! It was going to be another magical week on Rainspell Island!

RAINBOW magic™

THE MAGICAL CRAFTS FAIRIES

Rachel and Kirsty have found
Kayla's missing magic object. Now it's time
for them to help

Annabelle
the Drawing Fairy!

Join their next adventure
in this special sneak peek. . . .

Camp Breakfast

I think Rainspell Island is my favorite place in the whole world!" said Kirsty Tate, twirling on the spot.

Her best friend, Rachel Walker, jumped up and grabbed Kirsty's hands. They spun around in a circle until they both fell down on the grass, dizzy and happy. It was spring, and the campsite meadow was full of daisies and buttercups.

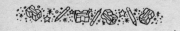

"The sun always shines on Rainspell Island," Rachel said, laughing.

Rainspell Island was the place where Rachel and Kirsty had first become friends — and where they began their adventures with the fairies! Now they were back again with their families for Crafts Week.

All week, the girls could take different classes in all sorts of arts and crafts, from painting to jewelry-making. On the final day, there was going to be an exhibition and competition with prizes! Everyone who had participated in Crafts Week could enter whatever they had made. Rachel and Kirsty couldn't wait!

"Breakfast!" called Mrs. Walker.

The girls raced back to the tent where the Walkers were staying. Mr. and Mrs.

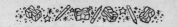

Walker sat outside the tent, cooking eggs, sausages, and home fries on their camp stove.

"It's a beautiful morning," said Mr. Walker. "I bet your parents wish they were camping, too, Kirsty."

Mr. and Mrs. Tate were staying in a local bed and breakfast, but Kirsty and Rachel had decided to have a sleepover in the tent so they wouldn't have to be separated.

"So, girls, which classes are you taking today?" asked Mrs. Walker.

It was the second day of Crafts Week, and there were lots of crafts that the girls wanted to try.

"We haven't decided yet," said Rachel, sitting down on a stool and holding out her plate for some breakfast. "What do

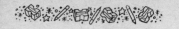

you think, Kirsty?"

Kirsty smiled and held out her own plate.

"There are so many to choose from, I can't make up my mind," she said.

Mr. and Mrs. Walker started to talk about an exhibition they wanted to see, and Kirsty leaned closer to her best friend.

"I wonder if we'll meet another fairy today," she whispered.

"I hope so," Rachel replied in a low voice. "There are still six magic objects to find, and we don't even know where to start looking!"

RAINBOW magic™

Which Magical Fairies Have You Met?

- ❑ The Rainbow Fairies
- ❑ The Weather Fairies
- ❑ The Jewel Fairies
- ❑ The Pet Fairies
- ❑ The Dance Fairies
- ❑ The Music Fairies
- ❑ The Sports Fairies
- ❑ The Party Fairies
- ❑ The Ocean Fairies
- ❑ The Night Fairies
- ❑ The Magical Animal Fairies
- ❑ The Princess Fairies
- ❑ The Superstar Fairies
- ❑ The Fashion Fairies
- ❑ The Sugar & Spice Fairies
- ❑ The Earth Fairies

■ SCHOLASTIC

Find all of your favorite fairy friends at
scholastic.com/rainbowmagic

HIT entertainment

RMFAIRY10

RAINBOW magic™

SPECIAL EDITION

Which Magical Fairies Have You Met?

3 stories in each one!

- ☐ Joy the Summer Vacation Fairy
- ☐ Holly the Christmas Fairy
- ☐ Kylie the Carnival Fairy
- ☐ Stella the Star Fairy
- ☐ Shannon the Ocean Fairy
- ☐ Trixie the Halloween Fairy
- ☐ Gabriella the Snow Kingdom Fairy
- ☐ Juliet the Valentine Fairy
- ☐ Mia the Bridesmaid Fairy
- ☐ Flora the Dress-Up Fairy
- ☐ Paige the Christmas Play Fairy
- ☐ Emma the Easter Fairy
- ☐ Cara the Camp Fairy
- ☐ Destiny the Rock Star Fairy
- ☐ Belle the Birthday Fairy
- ☐ Olympia the Games Fairy
- ☐ Selena the Sleepover Fairy
- ☐ Cheryl the Christmas Tree Fairy
- ☐ Florence the Friendship Fairy
- ☐ Lindsay the Luck Fairy
- ☐ Brianna the Tooth Fairy
- ☐ Autumn the Falling Leaves Fairy
- ☐ Keira the Movie Star Fairy
- ☐ Addison the April Fool's Day Fairy
- ☐ Bailey the Babysitter Fairy

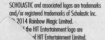

◼SCHOLASTIC

Find all of your favorite fairy friends at
scholastic.com/rainbowmagic

HIT entertainment

RMSPECIAL13